ideals®

CAREFREE DAYS

The clover days are summer days
　Of heavy-scented air,
Of ripening oats, high-reaching corn,
　And flowers everywhere.

　The clover days are carefree days,
　　The scent of new-mown hay,
　Of wading barefoot in the creek,
　　Of fair time underway.

The clover bloom is vital bloom
　That everyone adores,
A deep, delicious, grand perfume,
　The scent of all outdoors.

Craig E. Sathoff

Editorial Director, James Kuse

Managing Editor, Ralph Luedtke

Associate Editor, Colleen Callahan Gonring

Production Editor/Manager, Richard Lawson

Photographic Editor, Gerald Koser

Copy Editor, Sharon Style

Ideals (ISSN 0019-137X)

IDEALS—Vol. 36 No. 4 June MCMLXXIX, IDEALS (ISSN 0019-137X) is published eight times a year,
January, February, April, June, July, September, October, November
by IDEALS PUBLISHING CORPORATION, 11315 Watertown Plank Road, Milwaukee, Wis. 53226
Second class postage paid at Milwaukee, Wisconsin. Copyright © MCMLXXIX by IDEALS PUBLISHING CORPORATION.
All rights reserved. Title IDEALS registered U.S. Patent Office.
Published Simultaneously in Canada

ONE YEAR SUBSCRIPTION—eight consecutive issues as published—only $15.95
TWO YEAR SUBSCRIPTION—sixteen consecutive issues as published—only $27.95
SINGLE ISSUES—only $2.95

ISBN 0-89542-324-3 295

The Old Swimmin' Hole

Oh! the old swimmin' hole! whare the crick so still and deep
Looked like a baby-river that was laying half asleep,
And the gurgle of the worter round the drift jest below,
Sounded like the laugh of something we onc't ust to know
Before we could remember anything but the eyes
Of the angels lookin' out as we left Paradise;
But the merry days of youth is beyond our controle,
And it's hard to part ferever with the old swimmin' hole.

Oh! the old swimmin' hole! In the happy days of yore,
When I ust to lean above it on the old sickamore,
Oh! it showed me a face in its warm sunny tide
That gazed back at me so gay and glorified,
It made me love myself, as I leaped to caress
My shadder smilin' up at me with sich tenderness.

James Whitcomb Riley

Photograph Opposite
WILD ROSE, WISCONSIN
Ken Dequaine

The Country Maypole

It is a pleasant sight to see,
   A little village company
Drawn out upon the first of May
   To have their annual holiday;
The pole hung round with garlands gay,

   The young ones footing it away,
The aged cheering their old souls
   With recollecting their gambols,
Or, on the mirth and dancing failing,
   Their ofttimes-told old tales re-taleing.

Author Unknown

The May Day custom can be traced as far back as the ancient Romans who celebrated the rebirth of spring by decorating the temple of the goddess Flora with garlands. During medieval times, the English also had a custom of picking the hawthorn, which was named the "May," and the gathering of this flower termed "a-Maying." There were many festivities accompanying May Day; the entire population went "a-Maying," and they also selected a May queen, who was entertained with dancing, contests, and races. Another feature of May Day was the Maypole, which was decorated with garlands and colored ribbons. In fact, different towns competed with each other to claim the tallest Maypole. The Puritans, however, succeeded in having Maypoles banned until the reign of the Stuarts.

There is no one wild flower called the Mayflower. England has the hawthorn, Canada the wild lily of the valley, and the Pilgrims called the trailing arbutus the Mayflower.

Another custom associated with the Mayflower, is the giving of May baskets. It had been the custom to hang the basket on someone's door and run away before being caught; but nowadays, the giver wants to be recognized and have the favor returned. It has also become customary in schools and some of the supervised playgrounds to make up May baskets to give to hospital patients and the elderly.

Whatever the custom, May Day is celebrated with all the exuberance and gaiety befitting the rebirth of spring.

Shari Style

Summer Song

And the grass, the grass is tall, the grass is up for hay,
    With daisies white like silver and the buttercups like gold,
And it's oh! for once to play thro' the long, the lovely day,
    To laugh before the year grows old!

There are white moon daisies in the mist of the meadow
    Where the flowered grass scatters its seeds like spray,
There are purple Orchis by the wood-ways' shadow,
    There are pale dog roses by the white highways;

    There is silver moonlight on the breast of the river
        Where the willows tremble to the kiss of night,
    Where the nine tall aspens in the meadow shiver,
        Shiver in the night wind that turns them white.

And the lamps, the lamps are lit, the lamps the glowworms light,
    Between the silver aspens and the west's last gold.
And it's oh! to drink delight in the lovely lonely night,
    To be young before the heart grows old!

Edith Nesbit

Photograph Opposite
SALANO COUNTY, CALIFORNIA
Ed Cooper

James Whitcomb Riley

Born of pioneer stock in Greenfield, Indiana, in 1849, James Whitcomb Riley wrote simple down-home poetry, taking much from his own experiences in rural Indiana. He was so much loved, in fact, that in 1915 Indiana declared his birthday, October 7, an official state holiday. He was nicknamed the "Hoosier poet" and the "poet laureate of democracy." Working for the Indianapolis *Journal* (1877-85), he established himself in the literary world by contributing his verse to that newspaper. Riley had many honorary degrees given him, including receiving the gold medal of the National Institute of Arts and Letters, and being elected to the American Academy of Arts and Letters. Among his works are *The Old Swimmin' Hole and 'Leven More Poems, Little Orfant Annie Book*, and *When the Frost is on the Punkin*. Excerpts of his many works have appeared often in Ideals, for he captures the heart of the "days gone by."

Morning

Breath of morning, breath of May,
With your zest of yesterday
And crisp, balmy freshness, smite
Our old hearts with youth's delight.

Tilt the cap of boyhood, yea,
Where no "forelock" waves, today,
Back, in breezy, cool excess,
Stroke it with the old caress.

Let us see as we have seen,
Where all paths are dewy-green,
And all humankind are kin,
Let us be as we have been!

The Clover

Some sings of the lilly, and daisy, and rose,
And the pansies and pinks that the summertime throws
In the green grassy lap of the medder that lays
Blinkin' up at the skyes through the sunshiny days;
But what is the lilly and all of the rest
Of the flowers, to a man with a hart in his brest
That was dipped brimmin' full of the honey and dew
Of the sweet clover-blossoms his babyhood knew?

I never set eyes on a clover-field now,
Er fool round a stable, er climb in the mow,
But my childhood comes back jest as clear and as plane
As the smell of the clover I'm sniffin' again;

And I wunder away in a barefooted dream,
Whare I tangle my toes in the blossoms that gleam
With the dew of the dawn of the morning of love,
Ere it wept ore the graves that I'm weepin' above.

And so I love clover, it seems like a part
Of the sacerdest sorrows and joys of my hart;
And wharever it blossoms, oh, thare let me bow
And thank the good God as I'm thankin' him now;
And I pray to him still fer the stren'th when I die,
To go out in the clover and tell it good-by,
And lovin'ly nestle my face in its bloom
While my soul slips away on a breth of purfume.

The Days Gone By

O the days gone by! O the days gone by!
The apples in the orchard, and the pathway through the rye;
The chirrup of the robin, and the whistle of the quail
As he piped across the meadows, sweet as any nightingale;
When the bloom was on the clover, and the blue was in the sky,
And my happy heart brimmed over, in the days gone by.

In the days gone by, when my naked feet were tripped
By the honeysuckle tangles where the water lilies dipped,
And the ripples of the river lipped the moss along the brink
Where the placid-eyed and lazy-footed cattle came to drink,
And the tilting snipe stood fearless of the truant's wayward cry,
And the splashing of the swimmer, in the days gone by.

O the days gone by! O the days gone by!
The music of the laughing lip, the luster of the eye;
The childish faith in fairies, and Aladdin's magic ring,
The simple, soul-reposing, glad belief in every thing,
When life was like a story, holding neither sob nor sigh,
In the golden olden glory of the days gone by.

Nature

O nature! I do not aspire
To be the highest in thy choir,
　To be a meteor in thy sky,
　Or comet that may range on high;
Only a zephyr that may blow
Among the reeds by the river low;
　Give me thy most privy place
　Where to run my airy race.

In some withdrawn, unpublic mead
Let me sigh upon a reed,
　Or in the woods, with leafy din,
　Whisper the still evening in;
Some still work give me to do,
Only, be it near to you!

For I'd rather be thy child
And pupil, in the forest wild,
　Than be the king of men elsewhere,
　And most sovereign slave of care;
To have one moment of thy dawn,
Than share the city's year forlorn.

Henry David Thoreau

from The Planting of the Apple Tree

Come, let us plant the apple tree.
Cleave the tough greensward with the spade;
Wide let its hollow bed be made;
There gently lay the roots, and there
Sift the dark mould with kindly care,
And press it o'er them tenderly,
As, round the sleeping infants feet,
We softly fold the cradle-sheet;
So plant we the apple tree.

What plant we in this apple tree?
Buds, which the breath of summer days
Shall lengthen into leafy sprays;
Boughs where the thrush, with crimson breast,
Shall haunt, and sing, and hide her nest;
We plant, upon the sunny lea,
A shadow for the noontide hour,
A shelter from the summer shower,
When we plant the apple tree.

What plant we in this apple tree?
Sweets for a hundred flowery springs
To load the May-wind's restless wings,
When, from the orchard row, he pours
Its fragrance through our open doors;
A world of blossoms for the bee,
Flowers for the sick girl's silent room,
For the glad infant sprigs of bloom,
We plant with the apple tree.

What plant we in this apple tree?
Fruits that shall swell in sunny June,
And redden in the August noon,
And drop, when gentle airs come by,
That fan the blue September sky,
While children come, with cries of glee,
And seek them where the fragrant grass
Betrays their bed to those who pass,
At the foot of the apple tree.

Each year shall give this apple tree
A broader flush of roseate bloom,
A deeper maze of verdurous gloom,
And loosen, when the frost-clouds lower,
The crisp brown leaves in thicker shower.
The years shall come and pass, but we
Shall hear no longer, where we lie,
The summer's songs, the autumn's sigh,
In the boughs of the apple tree.

And time shall waste this apple tree.
Oh, when its aged branches throw
Thin shadows on the ground below,
Shall fraud and force and iron will
Oppress the weak and helpless still?
What shall the tasks of mercy be,
Amid the toils, the strifes, the tears
Of those who live when length of years
Is wasting this little apple tree?

"Who planted this old apple tree?"
The children of that distant day
Thus to some aged man shall say;
And, gazing on its mossy stem,
The gray-haired man shall answer them:
"A poet of the land was he,
Born in the rude but good old times;
'Tis said he made some quaint old rhymes,
On planting the apple tree."

William Cullen Bryant

Tell All the World

Tell all the world that summer's here again
  With song and joy; tell them, that they may know
How, on the hillside, in the shining fields
  New clumps of violets and daisies grow.

Tell all the world that summer's here again,
  That white clouds voyage through a sky so still
With blue tranquillity, it seems to hang
  One windless tapestry, from hill to hill.

Tell all the world that summer's here again:
  Folk go about so solemnly and slow,
Walking each one his grooved and ordered way
  I fear that, otherwise they will not know!

                                    Harry Kemp

My Haven

One day I spent an hour,
Just sitting in the sun,
I took in all the beauty,
Observed what God had done.

Aline Ubelhor

Carefree Way

Let's leave our cares and travel along
The sunny path of Carefree Way;
Let us pause and tarry here awhile,
Be joyous, happy while we may.

Clasp my hand, dear friend, and come with me,
And we will find a magic nook
Along some bubbling meadow stream,
Or by the fireside with a book.

Let's forget our cares and dream a bit,
There's happiness for you and me;
So just pass your happy thought along,
And walk the Carefree Way with me.

Elsie K. Pierce

Mountain Moment

Now it is just a dream. Short days ago
I stood entranced upon the earth's high rim,
There, where vast rolling cloud banks meet the snow
And life is full with overflowing brim.

Part of a dream, this fresh new world that flows
Like rich ambrosia surging through my veins;
Only the climber and the dreamer know
What high rewards the cautious heart disdains.

Now old familiar patterns mold the days—
Swift-rolling wheels have raced Time home once more,
And fifty weeks will know a hand that lays
One poignant finger on the heart's deep core.

There will be moments memory's trail leads high,
Half way to heaven, touching earth and sky.

Mary E. Linton

Summer Flowers

For only a brief time each year
   They show their lovely faces
In all the most unusual
   And unexpected places.

In valleys low, on highest hills,
   They somehow find their way
To spread beauty near and far
   In colorful display.

They offer a gift of fragrance
   That only summer blooms
Could bring in a blend of sweetness,
   The rarest of perfumes.

Some grow where none will ever see
   The loveliness they share,
But the glory of earth is greater
   For each one blooming there.

Virginia Katherine Oliver

Look Around

Look around a little
   At summertime's array;
Look around where gardens
   Are standing proud and gay;

Look where patterned shadows
   Fall across the lawn;
Look where dewdrops nestle
   Hours after dawn;

Look where skies are bluest,
   Where clouds are frothy white;
Look where sunsets linger
   Into the hours of night;

Look where trees stand quiet
   Or where they gently sway—
Look around a little,
   And love a summer day.

Lucille Veneklasen

Photograph opposite
FUSCHIA
Breta Westlund/TOM STACK
AND ASSOCIATES

Mothers

A mother is someone
    Dear to the heart,
Who's known you and loved you
    Right from the start.

She multiplies faith
    When problems are tough,
And divides up her love
    So each child has enough.

A mother reads stories
    Of dragons and kings.
She can build a great castle
    With boxes and things.

She teaches her children
    The alphabet
From a round oatmeal box
    Or a word-scramble set.

A mother is special
    To girls and to fellows.
She knows the right time
    To carry umbrellas.

She teaches good manners,
    Sews a fine seam,
Understands life,
    Believes in your dream.

A mother is memories
    Through rose-colored glass.
She's warm apple pie,
    A lady with class.

Her children go forth
    Insured with her prayers
And a truth universal:
    It's mother who cares.

Alice Leedy Mason

Fathers

A father is someone
    Precious and dear,
Whose faith in your efforts
    Eliminates fear.

You earn his respect;
    He's example and guide.
When the going gets rough,
    He stands by your side.

A father can help you
    With everyday things.
He can teach you to whistle,
    Build rubber-tire swings.

If you ask his opinion,
    He'll give you the facts.
He can teach you construction
    With a hammer and tacks.

A father knows problems
    May not be what they seem.
He's a very good listener,
    Believes in your dream.

He shows little interest
    In fashion or wealth;
Has a good sense of humor
    (He can laugh at himself).

A father is friendship
    In faded blue jeans.
He's a shoulder to cry on,
    The man with the means.

He has faith in tomorrow
    And strength from above.
In words spoken plainly,
    A father is love!

Alice Leedy Mason

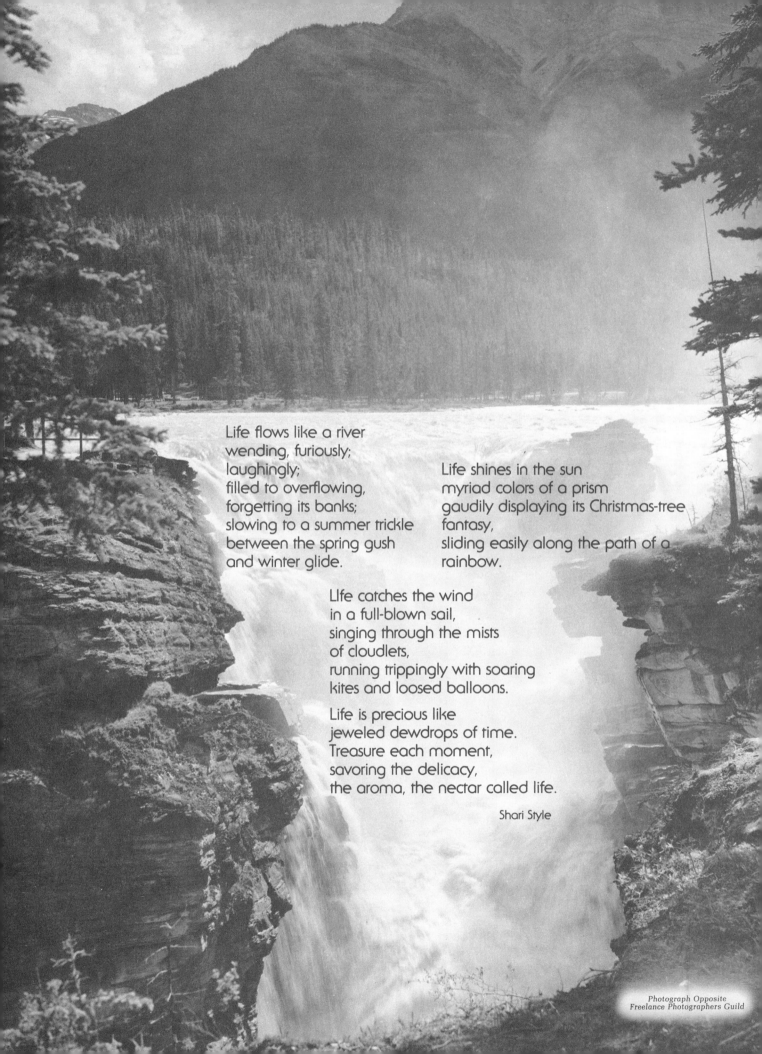

Life flows like a river
wending, furiously;
laughingly;
filled to overflowing,
forgetting its banks;
slowing to a summer trickle
between the spring gush
and winter glide.

Life shines in the sun
myriad colors of a prism
gaudily displaying its Christmas-tree
fantasy,
sliding easily along the path of a
rainbow.

LIfe catches the wind
in a full-blown sail,
singing through the mists
of cloudlets,
running trippingly with soaring
kites and loosed balloons.

Life is precious like
jeweled dewdrops of time.
Treasure each moment,
savoring the delicacy,
the aroma, the nectar called life.

Shari Style

That's Summer

Summer is freedom,
Laughter and joy;
Small pig-tailed darling,
Mischievous boy;
Shaded green valleys,
Streams running free;
Exploring the forest,
Climbing a tree.

Summer is dreaming,
Long lazy days;
Far-off horizons,
Flower strewn ways;
A whole wondrous world
All of us own;
Distant adventures,
Coming back home.

A small part of heaven
So much delight;
Fishin' and swimmin'
From dawn until night;
Hearts that are roaming,
Minds bright and free;
Eyes that know wonder,
That's summer to me.

Garnett Ann Schultz

My Garden Is a Pleasant Place

My garden is a pleasant place
Of sun glory and leaf grace.
There is an ancient cherry tree
Where yellow warblers sing to me,
And an old grape arbor, where
A robin builds her nest, and there
Above the lima beans and peas
She croons her little melodies,
Her blue eggs hidden in the green
Fastness of that leafy screen.
Here are striped zinnias that bees
Fly far to visit; and sweet peas,
Like little butterflies newborn,
And over by the tasseled corn
Are sunflowers and hollyhocks,
And pink and yellow four-o'clocks.
Here are hummingbirds that come
To seek the tall delphinium—
Songless bird and scentless flower
Communing in a golden hour.

There is no blue like the blue cup
The tall delphinium holds up,
Not sky, nor distant hill, nor sea,
Sapphire, nor lapis lazuli.
My lilac trees are old and tall;
I cannot reach their bloom at all.
They send their perfume over trees
And roofs and streets, to find the bees.

I wish some power would touch my ear
With magic touch, and make me hear
What all the blossoms say, and so
I might know what the winged things know.
I'd hear the sunflower's mellow pipe,
"Goldfinch, goldfinch, my seeds are ripe!"
I'd hear the pale wistaria sing,
"Moon moth, moon moth, I'm blossoming!"

I'd hear the evening primrose cry,
"Oh, firefly! come, firefly!"
And I would learn the jeweled word
The ruby-throated hummingbird
Drops into cups of larkspur blue,
And I would sing them all for you!

My garden is a pleasant place
Of moon glory and wind grace.
O friend, wherever you may be,
Will you not come to visit me?
Over fields and streams and hills,
I'll pipe like yellow daffodils,
And every little wind that blows
Shall take my message as it goes.
A heart may travel very far
To come where its desires are,
Oh, may some power touch my ear,
And grant me grace, and make you hear!

Louise Driscoll

Summer Joy

Let me wake in the early dawn,
   When the grass is flecked with dew,
And gather a basket of roses
   That will last the whole day through.

There's yellow and white, crimson and pink;
   Now my basket overflows.
I've captured the essence of summer,
   There in the heart of each rose.

Peggy Mlcuch

O Perfect Day

O perfect day, from your great treasury
   What may I take, what lovely, precious thing
To hold within my heart eternally?
   The glint of sunlight on a purple wing,
The love notes of a mating bird at dawn,
   The soft insistent murmur of the bees,
The crystal dewdrops sparkling on the lawn,
   The flickering shadows underneath the trees,
Nasturtiums flaming by an old stone wall,
The golden glory of a rose in bloom,
   The lilt of laughter ringing joyously,
My little children playing with their ball?
O perfect day, there is no room, no room—
   My heart could never hold such ecstasy.

Gwen Castle

Oh, I lose my heart
To each kitten I see;
I imagine they all
Are meant just for me.

And it matters not, if
They're fancy or plain,
They're equally precious
To me just the same.

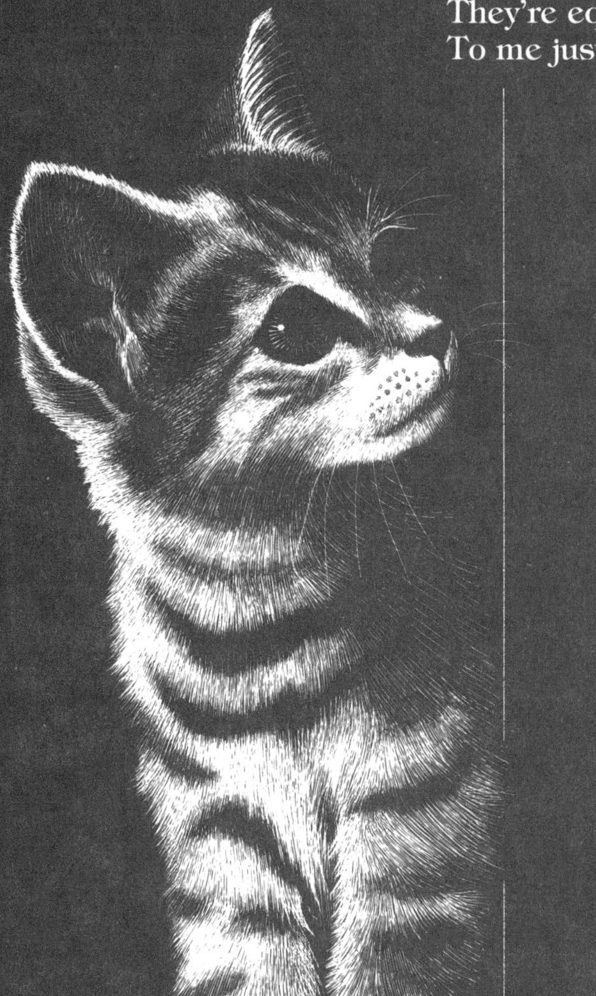

They capture my heart
With their come hither eyes;
And they break my heart
With their pitiful cries.

They're so silky and soft,
So cunning and sweet
As they scamper about,
Or doze at my feet.

They purr like angels
While impishly sitting
Just waiting their chance
To scatter my knitting!

No doubt about it, I'm
Thoroughly smitten
At very first sight
Of a cuddly kitten.

Mrs. Leon Randol

Photograph Opposite
Robert Cushman Hayes

The Wind

I saw you toss the kites on high
And blow the birds about the sky;
And all around I heard you pass,
Like ladies' skirts across the grass.
O wind, a-blowing all day long,
O wind, that sings so loud a song!

I saw the different things you did,
But always you, yourself, you hid.
I felt you push, I heard you call,
I could not see yourself at all.
O wind, a-blowing all day long,
O wind, that sings so loud a song!

O you that are so strong and cold,
O blower, are you young or old?
Are you a beast of field and tree,
Or just a stronger child than me?
O wind, a-blowing all day long,
O wind, that sings so loud a song!

Robert Louis Stevenson

The World's Music

The world's a very happy place,
Where every child should dance and sing,
And always have a smiling face,
And never sulk for anything.

I waken when the morning's come,
And feel the air, and light alive
With strange sweet music like the hum
Of bees about their busy hive.

The linnets play among the leaves
At hide-and-seek, and chirp and sing;
While, flashing to and from the eaves,
The swallows twitter on the wing.

The twigs that shake, and boughs that sway;
And tall old trees you could not climb;
And winds that come, but cannot stay,
Are gaily singing all the time.

Gabriel Setoun

Where Go the Boats?

Dark brown is the river,
   Golden is the sand,
It flows along for ever,
   With trees on either hand,

On goes the river
   And out past the mill,
Away down the valley,
   Away down the hill.

Green leaves a-floating,
   Castles of the foam,
Boats of mine a-boating—
   Where will all come home?

Away down the river,
   A hundred miles or more,
Other little children
   Shall bring my boats ashore.

Robert Louis Stevenson

Photograph Opposite
EGG HARBOR, WISCONSIN
Ken Dequaine

The Sand at the End of the Quay

Once upon a long ago
In a time that used to be,
On a shimmering strand
Of silvery sand
You sang to the wind and sea;
Sang a beautiful song
As you skipped along
Through the sand
In the shade
Near the sea,
You sang to the tide
Where the breakers glide
To crash on the rocks
On the quay;

You sang to the gulls
That circled high,
That rode the currents in the sky,
That swayed the trees
In a whispered hush,
At a time in your life
When there was no rush.

Now the sea sings to you
With its spray and its foam
And it calls you back
To your childhood home,
And you long to be
Back by the sea, in the sand
At the end of the quay.

                    Robert M. Kohler

Summer Sands

Sun-warmed sands of summertime
Carpeting the shores
Are times of happy wandering,
Exploring nature's shores!
A pebbly stone, a scallop shell
Of iridescent hue,
A sea gull's unearthed feather
Turned a silvery seascape blue;
The carefree summer hours
Spent beside a singing sea
Unlock a trove of treasures
And set our spirits free.

                    Catherine M. Acker

Painting Opposite
A HOLIDAY
by Edward Henry Potthast
The Art Institute of Chicago
Friends of American Art Collection

Summer Days

Soft green grass and babbling brooks,
A waterfall's glistening theme,
While Mother Nature paints for us
Summer's wildest dream.

A ribbon of moonlight in an evening sky,
A lonely breeze through cedars tall
Softly makes a rustling sound,
As it answers to the whippoorwill's call.

Silver dewdrops upon emerald trees,
Where the lovely songbird sings,
Helps to fill my heart with joy,
The happiness that summer brings.

Ellen Martin

The Pictorial Artistry of *Josef Muench*

The breathtaking scenic photography on the following pages is from the camera of Josef Muench, whose remarkable landscapes have been a part of Ideals for many years. Josef, born in Schweinfurt, Bavaria-Germany, came to the United States in 1928. His self-education in the field of photography began in his early teens when he roamed the Southwest deserts and mountains in search of meaningful subject matter. Josef possesses the rare, natural ability to visualize a picture before even raising the camera to his eye. He has covered many regions of the world, capturing the natural beauty of each for the enjoyment of all.

An Unknown Shore

As I stand on beautiful white beaches
And look with awe across the wide span of ocean,
I know a peace
Never felt anywhere else.

I marvel at palm trees
Swaying gently in the breeze.
I see the hand of the Creator
In the shells upon the sand.

I watch with wide-eyed wonder
As the white lace-edged waves
Rush to caress the shores,
Then swiftly descend once more.

My heart soars with the seagull,
And I long to sail away,
To explore an unknown shore
Far across this unknown sea.

Jean M. Drum

The Great Outdoors

This time of year turns the mind outdoors, to dream of
coming summer vacations in the wonderful realm of nature.

It's a beautiful world we live in—vast and varied in its scenic
splendor, where mountains, valleys, plains and deserts,
forests, jungles, tundras, rivers, lakes, and mighty seas form
a lovely backdrop and dwelling place for man and animal.

Esther York Burkholder

Photograph Opposite
HUAHINE, FRENCH POLYNESIA
Josef Muench

The Quiet Grandeur of the Petrified Forest

Petrified forest is a land of quiet grandeur, a place of contrasts and change. It contains some of the largest petrified logs in the world, but you may best remember the exquisite color and pattern of a tiny chip of petrified wood. The park preserves the greatest concentration of petrified wood known to man, but a delicately balanced pedestal log may be more impressive than thousands of petrified logs scattered over acres of land. The endlessly varied hues of the Painted Desert (which makes up about half of the park) are a treat to road weary eyes, and the patterns of these intricately carved badlands are bewilderingly complex. The chances are that you will see no water in the park, but nearly all you see will have been produced by the action of water in geologically recent years. Short trails can take you from the sound of the road to the quiet of the hills. Park Rangers will help you plan a longer hike into the Painted Desert Wilderness, where little has changed in thousands of years.

From a parking lot filled with modern cars, walk a thousand years into the past when ancient man made his home here. Just for fun, "read" the ancient petroglyphs that your predecessors here chipped into sandstone slabs. Deliberate a little on why there are only ruins here today, why man no longer builds pueblos here and why the Indians no longer farm the land. Give some thought to what this might mean to you, and to your descendants.

Petrified Forest offers to visitors an exercise in serendipity, the art of finding greater value in an activity than one would expect. What may start as a reluctant break in the high speed trip from one place to another, often develops into a totally new and different experience. To the visitor who takes the time to enjoy the park, rather than just "seeing" it, the few hours lost in the hectic rush to "see" another place are more than repaid. . . .

Man has known Petrified Forest for over 1500 years, and early man apparently was well adapted to its conditions. More than 300 Indian ruins are located in the park. Not all of these were occupied at the same time, and they range in size from one room shelters to the 150 room pueblo on the Puerco River. No men lived here when the Spanish first explored the Southwest in 1540, and few have lived here since. . . .

The early residents of what is now Petrified Forest National Park lived in close harmony with their surroundings. Most pottery, tools, houses, and clothing were fashioned from local materials. . . . Foods were limited to plants that could be grown in this climate and animals that lived here and could be captured. . . . Man's continued existence depended upon there being no drastic environmental changes of long duration. . . .

. . . Farming in many places became impossible, and the human population in those places could no longer continue. . . . The great cliff dwellings and hundreds of other communities in the Southwest were deserted and have never been reoccupied.

In the Petrified Forest area, the extended period of drought brought one way of life to an end and stimulated the development of new fashions. As their environment changed, the Indians adapted to the changes by developing new farming methods, new styles of construction, and other new customs. . . .

. . . the climate [of Petrified Forest] is one of extremes and occasional violence. The annual precipitation averages only about nine inches . . . and half of it comes in short violent thunderstorms in July, August, and September. . . . May, June, and sometimes early July are typically very dry. About half of the year's precipitation is received in showers and snow scattered throughout the rest of the year. . . . Sub-zero temperatures are not uncommon on winter nights . . . even in mid-winter, however, moderate afternoon temperatures are not unusual. . . . the temperature rises to 100° or very slightly higher on just a few days in July and averages in the low 90's for much of the summer.

Environmental adaptations seem endlessly varied. . . . Changes in the environment usually take place gradually over very long periods. Successive generations of plants and animals adjust to minor changes in their life times. . . . When environmental changes exceed a species' limit of toleration, however, that species dies. . . .

[Today, man is changing this environment too rapidly for many species to adapt. Technology exists to reverse this present trend, but only by educating citizens to our political, financial, industrial, and personal responsibilities. We are all involved, either in the conservation or the oblivion of our natural heritage and national parks.]

Photograph Opposite
PETRIFIED FOREST NATIONAL PARK, ARIZONA
Ed Cooper

My Dog

He's jus' a plain dog like you see everyday—
A dog that is willing to romp an' to play,
An' all that he wants is for me to know
That he'll be my friend wherever we go.

In fun he will bark, but he never will fail
To show true friendship with a wag of his tail,
An' no matter what happens, no faith will he hide,
As with loyalty an' courage, he walks by my side.

When a cat comes round,
A streak you will see
As he starts in
Chasing it up a tree,
An' he'll hang his head
When I call, "Come along!"
'Cause he knows very well
That he's done something wrong.
Through the woods he will hunt
To his heart's content,
'Till he's all tir'd out
An' his strength is spent,
An' when his frolic is done,
By the fire he'll lay,
Ever willing to rest
An' to call it a day.

P. F. Freeman

A little girl should have a swing
  Beneath an apple tree in spring,
Where she can make believe that she
  Is floating through a petalled sea,

Up to the stars, and farther still,
  Beyond each blue and distant hill
And into a golden wonderland
  That only a child can understand.

Alice MacKenzie Swaim

The Swing

How do you like to go up in a swing,
   Up in the air so blue?
"Oh, I do think it the pleasantest thing
   Ever a child can do!"

"Up in the air and over the wall,
   Till I can see so wide,
Rivers and trees and cattle and all
   Over the countryside—

"Till I look down on the garden green
   Down on the roof so brown—
Up in the air I go flying again,
   Up in the air and down!"

Robert Louis Stevenson

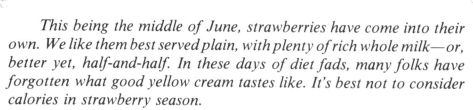

This being the middle of June, strawberries have come into their own. We like them best served plain, with plenty of rich whole milk—or, better yet, half-and-half. In these days of diet fads, many folks have forgotten what good yellow cream tastes like. It's best not to consider calories in strawberry season.

For a change, I sometimes serve strawberry shortcake. We like a biscuit dough, slightly sweetened and made with plenty of shortening. The dough is patted into shape in two round cake pans, covered generously with melted butter, and baked until done. One layer is put into a glass baking dish, covered with strawberries which have previously been washed and sweetened; then the other layer is put on top and berries are piled about it as high as the dish will permit. The shortcake is served slightly warm.

"Ummmm! Good!" as the children say.

Wild strawberries are plentiful, too. Out in the woods and along the railroad one may gather a quart in seemingly no time at all.

May Allread Baker

STRAWBERRY SHORTCAKE

2¼ c. cake flour
 4 t. baking powder
 2 T. sugar
 ½ t. salt
 ⅓ c. shortening
 1 egg, slightly beaten
 ⅔ c. milk

Sift flour, baking powder, salt, and sugar together. Add shortening, cutting in with pastry blender until crumbly. Stir in egg and milk. Spread in greased 8-inch round cake pan. Bake in a 425° oven for 15 minutes.

TOPPING

 2 pts. fresh strawberries
 1 c. sugar
 ½ c. heavy cream
 1 t. vanilla

Wash, hull, and slice strawberries into a medium bowl. Gently stir in sugar. Let stand. In a small bowl, whip cream. Add vanilla. Split shortcake. Place on serving platter cut side up. Spoon half of strawberry mixture on the cake. Top with other half of shortcake, cut side down. Add remaining berries and cream.

Children's Day

The world would be a dismal place without the laughter, joy, and innocent antics of playing children. The needs and interests of our children should be of primary concern every day, but many times they are overlooked because of the problems and pressures presented in day-to-day living. Therefore, in many Christian churches throughout the United States, the second Sunday in June has long been celebrated as Children's Day.

It is believed the custom of devoting a special day to the interests and needs of the young can be traced back to the Old World May Day rite, during which children carried flowers and tree branches to churches when they were confirmed into their faiths. The earliest known celebration of a special Children's Day in the United States took place in Chelsea, Massachusettes, on the second Sunday in June 1856, to commemorate the training of children in Christian living.

The institution of Children's Day has become an important church festival in many areas. It is a time when the special needs of our young people and their importance as the future supporters and leaders of our churches and communities are recognized, emphasized, and celebrated. In keeping with this recognition, the concern for a deeper understanding of the special needs of children has reached the center of world attention. And to mark the twentieth anniversary of the Declaration of the Rights of the Child, the United Nations has proclaimed 1979 as International Year of the Child. In this special year, we should all take to heart the special problems in the development of our most precious possessions, our children.

David Schansberg

The Soul of a Child

The soul of a child is the loveliest flower
That grows in the Garden of God.
Its climb is from weakness to knowledge and power,
To the sky from the clay to the clod.
To beauty and sweetness it grows under care,
Neglected, 'tis ragged and wild.
'Tis a plant that is tender, but wondrously rare,
The sweet wistful soul of a child.

Be tender, O Gardener, and give it its share
Of moisture, of warmth and of light,
And let it not lack for the painstaking care
To protect it from frost and from blight.
A glad day will come when its bloom shall unfold,
It will seem that an Angel has smiled,
Reflecting a beauty and sweetness untold
In the sensitive soul of a child.

Author Unknown

The Mountain Canyon

Here is such dark cool beauty, such clear sound:
An echo runs along the far-off heights
Like crystal striking crystal. Seaward bound
The mountain torrent, filled with silver lights,
Makes wild protest; and a trodden twig somewhere
Breaks, and the sound is loud upon the air.

An aspen quakes beside a waterfall.
The pines climb skyward, not a branch is stirred,
The blue spruce lifts against the canyon wall,
And now a dark bough dips where a crimson bird
With iridescent wings and breast of flame
Swings, and calls to his mate a singing name.

Deep in a dark cool tree a fiery bird
Has written a poem without pen or word.

Grace Noll Crowell

THE MOUNTAIN CANYON from THE ETERNAL THINGS: THE BEST OF
GRACE NOLL CROWELL (1977). Copyright 1942 by Harper & Row, Publishers, Inc.; renewed, 1970 by Reid Crowell. By permission of the publisher.

Photograph Opposite
EL CAPITAN
YOSEMITE VALLEY
Ed Cooper

What Is So Rare As a Day In June

James Russell Lowell
From "The Vision of Sir Launfal"

And what is so rare as a day in June?
  Then, if ever, come perfect days;
Then heaven tries the earth if it be in tune,
  And over it softly her warm ear lays:
Whether we look, or whether we listen,
  We hear life murmur, or see it glisten;
Every clod feels a stir of might,
  An instinct within it that reaches and towers,
And, groping blindly above it for light,
  Climbs to a soul in grass and flowers;
The flush of life may well be seen
  Thrilling back over hills and valleys;
The cowslip startles in meadows green,
  The buttercup catches the sun in its chalice,
And there's never a leaf nor a blade too mean
  To be some happy creature's palace;
The little bird sits at his door in the sun,
  Atilt like a blossom among the leaves,
And lets his illumined being o'errun
  With the deluge of summer it receives;
His mate feels the eggs beneath her wings,
  And the heart in her dumb breast flutters and sings;
He sings to the wide world, and she to her nest,—
  In the nice ear of nature which song is the best?

Now is the high tide of the year,
  And whatever of life hath ebbed away
Comes flooding back, with a ripply cheer,
  Into every bare inlet and creek and bay;
Now the heart is so full that a drop overfills it,
  We are happy now because God wills it;
No matter how barren the past may have been,
  'Tis enough for us now that the leaves are green;
We sit in the warm shade and feel right well
  How the sap creeps up and the blossoms swell;
We may shut our eyes, but we cannot help knowing
  That skies are clear and grass is growing;
The breeze comes whispering in our ear,
  That dandelions are blossoming near,
That maize has sprouted, that streams are flowing,
  That the river is bluer than the sky,
That the robin is plastering his house hard by;
  And if the breeze kept the good news back,
For other couriers we should not lack;
  We could guess it all by yon heifer's lowing,
And hark! how clear bold chanticleer,
  Warmed with the new wine of the year,
Tells all in his lusty crowing!

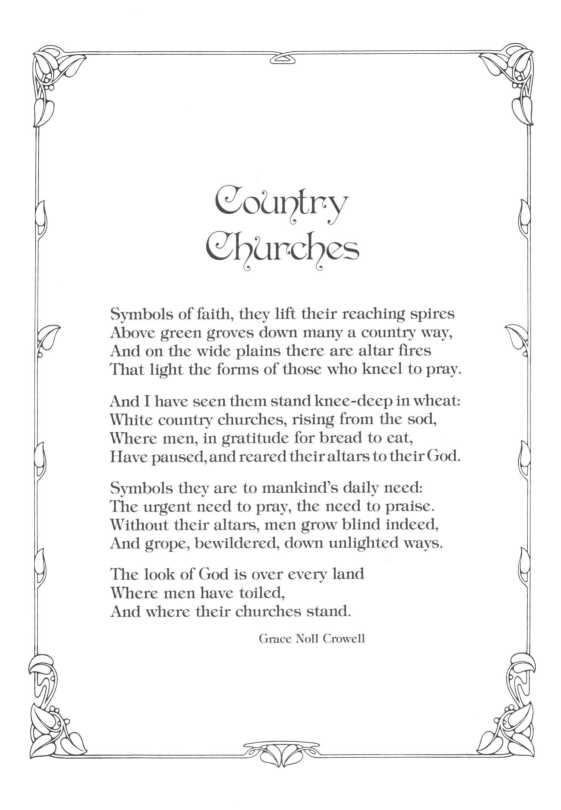

Country Churches

Symbols of faith, they lift their reaching spires
Above green groves down many a country way,
And on the wide plains there are altar fires
That light the forms of those who kneel to pray.

And I have seen them stand knee-deep in wheat:
White country churches, rising from the sod,
Where men, in gratitude for bread to eat,
Have paused, and reared their altars to their God.

Symbols they are to mankind's daily need:
The urgent need to pray, the need to praise.
Without their altars, men grow blind indeed,
And grope, bewildered, down unlighted ways.

The look of God is over every land
Where men have toiled,
And where their churches stand.

Grace Noll Crowell

COUNTRY CHURCHES from THE ETERNAL THINGS: THE BEST OF
GRACE NOLL CROWELL (1977). Copyright, 1930 by Harper & Row, Publishers, Inc.; renewed, 1958 by Grace Noll Crowell. By permission of the
publisher.

The Child Next Door

The child next door has a wreath on her hat;
Her afternoon frock sticks out like that,
    All soft and frilly;
She doesn't believe in fairies at all
(She told me over the garden wall)—
    She thinks they're silly.

      The child next door has a watch of her own;
      She has shiny hair and her name is Joan;
          (Mine's only Mary.)
      But doesn't it seem very sad to you
      To think that she never her whole life through
          Has seen a fairy?

                  Rose Fyleman

A Summer Day

The sun shone in the valley
And across the summer hill,
With rays of golden splendor
While the world was calm and still;
The little birds were singing
Songs of happiness and cheer,
And my heart was filled with gladness,
At this special time of year.

The oak tree cast a shadow
With her friendly spreading arms,
And a hummingbird so precious
Seemed entranced with nature's charms;
A cloud as soft as cotton
Found its way across the sky,
And a warm breeze whispered softly
As it slowly floated by.

The day was so inviting
In this cherished country nook;
And I seemed to hear the babbling
Of the far-off little brook.
The grass as smooth as velvet,
Made a pillow for my head;
And my eyes could see the cloud steps
Where the little angels tread.

The sun shone in the valley
And my heart held priceless joy
On this lovely day in summer,
Just so precious to enjoy;
A world of quiet beauty,
In a quaint and charming way,
Everything your heart could ask for
In one gorgeous summer day.

Garnett Ann Schultz

On the following three pages we are presenting an excerpt from the children's classic, *Toby Tyler or Ten Weeks with a Circus*. Toby, who lives with his Uncle Daniel, visits a circus and is offered a job by the candy vendor, Mr. Lord. The boy accepts the position gladly and, during his stay with the circus, meets up with many interesting characters, including Mr. Stubbs, a monkey who becomes a good friend. Toby's boss, however, proves to be anything but a friend; and Toby begins to regret his hasty decision to leave home. He has thoughts of running away once again, only this time back to his Uncle whom he discovers he truly misses and loves. Much to Toby's surprise, he finds that Uncle Daniel missed him, too. Toby's adventures with the circus, as told by author James Otis, are heartwarming and exciting; and, as the novel unfolds, we see a young boy realize just what running away from home really means.

Toby Runs Away from Home

Toby could scarcely restrain himself at the prospect of this golden future that had so suddenly opened before him. He tried to express his gratitude, but could only do so by evincing his willingness to commence work at once.

"No, no, that won't do," said Mr. Lord, cautiously. "If your uncle Daniel should see you working here, he might mistrust something, and then you couldn't get away."

"I don't believe he'd try to stop me," said Toby, confidently; "for he's told me lots of times that it was a sorry day for him when he found me."

"We won't take any chances, my son," was the reply, in a very benevolent tone, as he patted Toby on the head and at the same time handed him a piece of pasteboard. "There's a ticket for the circus, and you come around to see me about ten o'clock tonight. I'll put you on one of the wagons, and by tomorrow morning your uncle Daniel will have hard work to find you. . . . "

. . . That night—despite the fact that he was going to travel with the circus, despite the fact that his home was not a happy or cheerful one—Toby was not in a pleasant frame of mind. He began to feel for the first time that he was doing wrong; and as he gazed at Uncle Daniel's stern, forbidding-looking face, it seemed to have changed somewhat from its severity, and caused a great lump of something to come up in his throat as he thought that perhaps he should never see it again. Just then one or two kind words would have prevented him from running away, bright as the prospect of circus life appeared. . . .

. . . Still, he had no thought of breaking the engagement which he had made. He went to his room, made a bundle of his worldly possessions, and crept out of the back door, down the road to the circus.

Mr. Lord saw him as soon as he arrived on the grounds, and as he passed another ticket to Toby he took his bundle from him, saying, as he did so: "I'll pack up your bundle with my things, and then you'll be sure not to lose it. Don't you want some candy?"

Toby shook his head; he had just discovered that there was possibly some connection between his heart and his stomach, for his grief at leaving home had taken from him all desire for good things. It is also more than possible that Mr. Lord had had experience enough with boys to know that they might be homesick on the eve of starting to travel with a circus; and in order to make sure that Toby would keep to his engagement he was unusually kind. . . .

The First Day with the Circus

" . . . I want him to go to work and wash the tumblers, and fix up the things in that green box, so we can commence to sell as soon as we get into town," snarled Mr. Lord, as he motioned toward a large green chest that had been taken out of one of the carts, and which Toby saw was filled with dirty glasses, spoons, knives, and other utensils such as were necessary to carry on the business. . . .

. . . He was obliged to bring water, to cut up the lemons, fetch and carry fruit from the booth in the big tent to the booth on the outside, until he was ready to drop with fatigue, and, having had no time for breakfast, was nearly famished.

It was quite noon before he was permitted to go to the hotel for something to eat, and then Ben's advice to be one of the first to get to the tables was not needed. . . .

. . . Toby could not understand what it was that Mr. Lord said, but he could understand that his employer was angry at somebody or something, and he tried unusually hard to please him. He talked to the boys who had gathered around, to induce them to buy, washed the glasses as fast as they were used, tried to keep off the flies, and in every way he could think of endeavored to please his master . . .

. . . It was as if he had suddenly seen one of the boys from home, and Toby, uttering an exclamation of delight, ran up to the cage and put his hand through the wires.

The monkey, in the gravest possible manner, took one of the fingers in his paw, and Toby shook hands with him very earnestly.

"I was sorry that I couldn't speak to you when I went in this noon," said Toby, as if making an apology; "but, you see, there were so many around here to see you that I couldn't get the chance. Did you see me wink at you?"

The monkey made no reply, but he twisted his face into such a funny little grimace that Toby was quite as well satisfied as if he had spoken.

"I wonder if you hain't some relation to Steve Stubbs?" Toby continued, earnestly, "for you look just like him, only he don't have quite so many whiskers. What I wanted to say was that I'm awful sorry I run away. I used to think that Uncle Dan'l was bad enough; but he was just a perfect good Samarathon to what Mr. Lord an' Mr. Jacobs are; an' when Mr. Lord looks at me with that crooked eye of his I feel it 'way down in my boots. Do you know"—and here Toby put his mouth nearer to the monkey's head and whispered—"I'd run away from this circus if I could get the chance. Wouldn't you?"

Just at this point, as if in answer to the question, the monkey stood up on his hind feet and reached out his paw to the boy, who seemed to think this was his way of being more emphatic in saying "Yes."

Toby took the paw in his hand, shook it again earnestly, and said, as he released it: "I was pretty sure you felt just about the same way I did, Mr. Stubbs, when I passed you this noon. Look here"—and Toby took the money from his pocket which had been given him—"I got all that this afternoon, an' I'll try an' stick it out somehow till I get as much as ten dollars, an' then we'll run away some night, an' go 'way off as far as—as—as out West; an' we'll stay there, too. . . ."

. . . Toby knew that the Living Skeleton was before him, and his big brown eyes opened all the wider as he gazed at him.

"What is the matter, little fellow?" asked the man, in a kindly tone. "What makes you cry so? Has Job been up to his old tricks again?"

"I don't know what his old tricks are"—and Toby sobbed, the tears coming again because of the sympathy which this man's voice expressed for him—"but I know that he's a mean, ugly thing—that's what I know; an' if I could only get back to Uncle Dan'l, there hain't elephants enough in all the circuses in the world to pull me away again."

"Oh, you run away from home, did you?"

"Yes, I did," sobbed Toby, "an' there hain't any boy in any Sunday-school book that ever I read that was half so sorry he'd been bad as I am. It's awful; an' now I can't have any supper, 'cause I stopped to talk with Mr. Stubbs."

"Is Mr. Stubbs one of your friends?" asked the skeleton, as he seated himself in Mr. Lord's own private chair. . . .

"Yes, he is, an' he's the only one in this whole circus who 'pears to be sorry for me.

Mr. Castle Teaches Toby to Ride

" . . . I want you to go in an' see Mr. Castle; he's goin' to show you how to ride," said Mr. Lord, in as kindly a tone as if he were conferring some favor on the boy.

If Toby had dared to, he would have rebelled then and there and refused to go; but, as he hadn't the courage for such proceeding, he walked meekly into the tent and toward the ring. . . .

When Toby got within sight of the ring he was astonished at what he saw. A horse, with a broad wooden saddle, was being led slowly around the ring; Mr. Castle was standing on one side, with a long whip in his hand; and on the tent pole, which stood in the center of the ring, was a long arm, from which dangled a leathern belt attached to a long rope that was carried through the end of the arm and run down to the base of the pole.

. . . Toby's first lesson with Mr. Castle was the most pleasant one he had; for after the boy had once been into the ring his master seemed to expect that he could do everything which he was told to do, and when he failed in any little particular the long lash of the whip would go curling around his legs or arms, until the little fellow's body and limbs were nearly covered with the blue-and-black stripes. . . .

Toby's First Appearance in the Ring

When the circus entered the town which had been selected as the place where Toby was to make his debut as a circus rider the boy noticed a new poster among the many glaring and gaudy bills which set forth the varied and numerous attractions that were to be found under one canvas for a trifling admission fee, and he noticed it with some degree of interest, not thinking for a moment that it had any reference to him.

. . . The music struck up, the horses cantered around the ring, and Toby had really started as a circus rider.

"Remember," said Ella to him, in a low tone, just as the horses started, "you told me that you would ride just as well as you could, and we must earn the dollars mamma promised."

It seemed to Toby at first as if he could not stand up, but by the time they had ridden around the ring once, and Ella had again cautioned him against making any mistake, for the sake of the money which they were going to earn, he was calm and collected enough to carry out his part of the "act" as well as if he had been simply taking a lesson.

The act consisted in their riding side by side, jumping over banners and through hoops covered with paper, and then the most difficult portion began.

The saddles were taken off the horses, and they were to ride first on one horse and then on the other, until they concluded their performance by riding twice around the ring side by side, standing on their horses, each one with a hand on the other's shoulder.

All this was successfully accomplished without a single error, and when they rode out of the ring the applause was so great as to leave no doubt but that they would be recalled and thus earn the promised money. . . .

Off for Home!

. . . Under all these pressing attentions it was some time before Toby found a chance to say that which he had come to say, and when he did he was almost at a loss how to proceed; but at last he commenced by starting abruptly on his subject with the words, "I've made up my mind to leave tonight."

"Leave tonight?" repeated the skeleton, inquiringly, not for a moment believing that Toby could think of running away after the brilliant success he had just made. "What do you mean, Toby?"

"Why, you know that I've been wantin' to get away from the circus," said Toby, a little impatient that his friend should be so wonderfully stupid, "an' I think that I'll have as good a chance now as ever I shall, so I'm goin' to try it."

"Bless us!" exclaimed the fat lady, in a gasping way. "You don't mean to say that you're goin' off just when you've started in the business so well? I thought you'd want to stay after you'd been so well received this afternoon."

"No," said Toby—and one quick little sob popped right up from his heart and out before he was aware of it—"I learned to ride because I had to, but I never give up runnin' away. I must see Uncle Dan'l, an' tell him how sorry I am for what I did; an' if he won't have anything to say to me I'll come back; but if he'll let me I'll stay there, an' I'll be *so* good that by 'n' by he'll forget that I run off an' left him without sayin' a word."

Home and Uncle Daniel

. . . When he entered the old familiar sitting-room Uncle Daniel was seated near the window, alone, looking out wistfully—as Toby thought —across the fields of yellow waving grain.

Toby crept softly in, and, going up to the old man, knelt down and said, very humbly, and with his whole soul in the words, "Oh, Uncle Dan'l! if you'll only forgive me for bein' so wicked an' runnin' away, an' let me stay here again—for it's all the home I ever had—I'll do everything you tell me to, an' never whisper in meetin' or do anything bad."

And then he waited for the words which would seal his fate. They were not long in coming.

"My poor boy," said Uncle Daniel, softly, as he stroked Toby's refractory red hair, "my love for you was greater than I knew, and when you left me I cried aloud to the Lord as if it had been my own flesh and blood that had gone afar from me. Stay here, Toby, my son, and help to support this poor old body as it goes down into the dark valley of the shadow of death; and then, in the bright light of that glorious future, Uncle Daniel will wait to go with you into the presence of Him who is ever a father to the fatherless."

And in Uncle Daniel's kindly care we may safely leave Toby Tyler.

James Otis

The Little League

A wonderful organization
Held in high esteem;
It is the special answer
To a small boy's dream.

For here he dons a baseball cap,
And here he's ten feet tall;
He takes his place on the team;
The ump yells, "Play ball."

His eyes are bright, his heart is true,
His arms and legs are strong,
And he is cheered and urged to win
By the watching throng.

Throughout the game he tries his best,
His skilled hands streaked with dirt,
He grins and wipes his freckled face
And always keeps alert.

Though just a boy, he proves to all
He really is a man,
By playing fair and square to win
And does the best he can.

LaVerne P. Larson

Photograph Opposite
Jack Zehrt

The Barefoot Boy

John Greenleaf Whittier

Blessings on thee, little man,
Barefoot boy, with cheek of tan!
With thy turned-up pantaloons,
And thy merry whistled tunes;
With thy red lip, redder still
Kissed by strawberries on the hill;
With the sunshine on thy face,
Through thy torn brim's jaunty grace;
From my heart I give thee joy;
I was once a barefoot boy!

Prince thou art, the grown-up man
Only is republican.
Let the million-dollared ride!
Barefoot, trudging at his side,
Thou hast more than he can buy
In the reach of ear and eye,
Outward sunshine, inward joy;
Blessings on thee, barefoot boy!

Oh, for boyhood's painless play,
Sleep that wakes in laughing day,
Health that mocks the doctor's rules,
Knowledge, never learned of schools,
Of the wild bee's morning chase,
Of the wild flower's time and place,
Flight of fowl and habitude
Of the tenants of the wood;
How the tortoise bears his shell,
How the woodchuck digs his cell,
And the ground-mole sinks his well;
How the robin feeds her young,
How the oriole's nest is hung;
Where the whitest lilies blow,
Where the freshest berries grow,

Where the ground nut trails its vine,
Where the wood-grape's clusters shine;
Of the black wasp's cunning way,
Mason of his walls of clay,
And the architectural plans
Of gray hornet artisans!
For, eschewing books and tasks,
Nature answers all he asks;
Hand in hand with her he walks,
Face to face with her he talks,
Part and parcel of her joy,
Blessings on the barefoot boy!

Oh, for boyhood's time of June,
Crowding years in one brief moon,
When all things I heard or saw,
Me, their master, waited for.
I was rich in flowers and trees,
Hummingbirds and honeybees;
For my sport the squirrel played,
Plied the snouted mole his spade;
For my taste the blackberry cone
Purpled over hedge and stone;
Laughed the brook for my delight
Through the day and through the night,
Whispering at the garden wall,
Talked with me from fall to fall;
Mine the sand-rimmed pickerel pond,

Mine the walnut slopes beyond,
Mine, on bending orchard trees,
Apples of Hesperides!
Still as my horizon grew,
Larger grew my riches too;
All the world I saw or knew
Seemed a complex Chinese toy,
Fashioned for a barefoot boy!

Oh, for festal dainties spread,
Like my bowl of milk and bread;
Pewter spoon and bowl of wood,
On the doorstone, gray and rude!
O'er me, like a regal tent,
Cloudy-ribbed, the sunset bent,
Purple-curtained, fringed with gold,
Looped in many a wind-swung fold;
While for music came the play
Of the pied frogs' orchestra;
And, to light the noisy choir,
Lit the fly his lamp of fire.
I was monarch: pomp and joy
Waited on the barefoot boy!

Cheerily, then, my little man,
Live and laugh, as boyhood can!
Though the flinty slopes be hard,
Stubble-speared the new-mown sward,
Every morn shall lead thee through
Fresh baptisms of the dew;
Every evening from thy feet
Shall the cool wind kiss the heat:
All too soon these feet must hide
In the prison cells of pride,
Lose the freedom of the sod,
Like a colt's for work be shod,
Made to tread the mills of toil,
Up and down in ceaseless moil:
Happy if their track be found
Never on forbidden ground;
Happy if they sink not in
Quick and treacherous sands of sin.
Ah! that thou couldst know thy joy,
Ere it passes, barefoot boy!

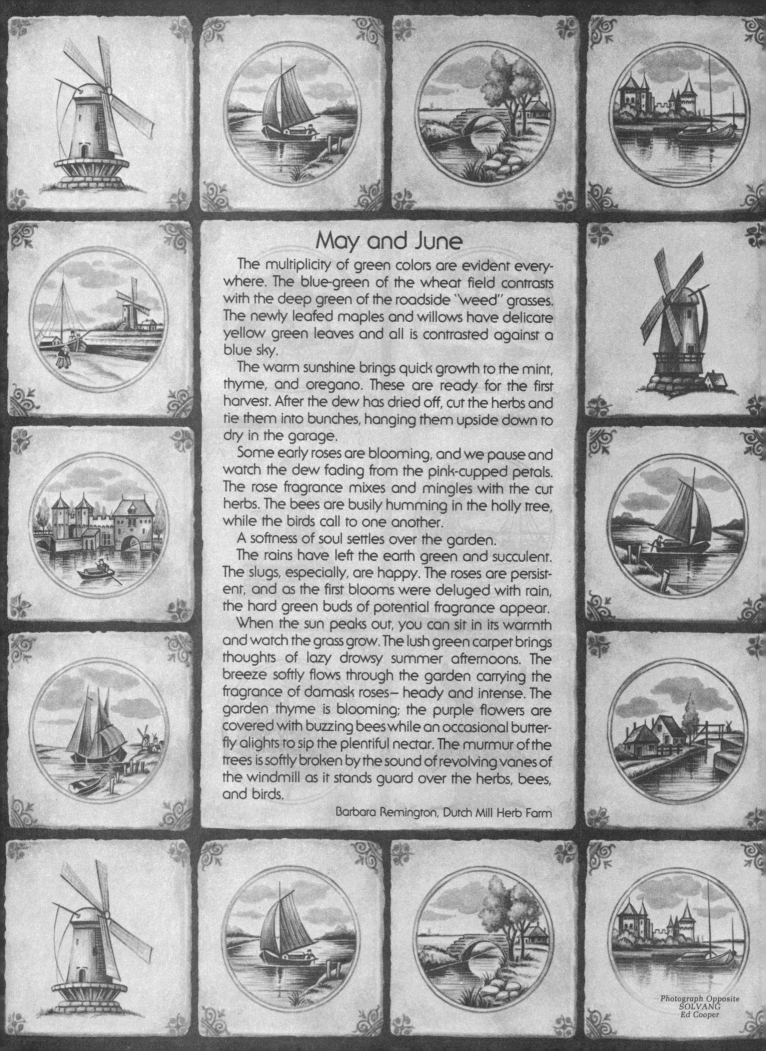

May and June

The multiplicity of green colors are evident everywhere. The blue-green of the wheat field contrasts with the deep green of the roadside "weed" grasses. The newly leafed maples and willows have delicate yellow green leaves and all is contrasted against a blue sky.

The warm sunshine brings quick growth to the mint, thyme, and oregano. These are ready for the first harvest. After the dew has dried off, cut the herbs and tie them into bunches, hanging them upside down to dry in the garage.

Some early roses are blooming, and we pause and watch the dew fading from the pink-cupped petals. The rose fragrance mixes and mingles with the cut herbs. The bees are busily humming in the holly tree, while the birds call to one another.

A softness of soul settles over the garden.

The rains have left the earth green and succulent. The slugs, especially, are happy. The roses are persistent, and as the first blooms were deluged with rain, the hard green buds of potential fragrance appear.

When the sun peaks out, you can sit in its warmth and watch the grass grow. The lush green carpet brings thoughts of lazy drowsy summer afternoons. The breeze softly flows through the garden carrying the fragrance of damask roses— heady and intense. The garden thyme is blooming; the purple flowers are covered with buzzing bees while an occasional butterfly alights to sip the plentiful nectar. The murmur of the trees is softly broken by the sound of revolving vanes of the windmill as it stands guard over the herbs, bees, and birds.

Barbara Remington, Dutch Mill Herb Farm

Photograph Opposite
SOLVANG
Ed Cooper

Butternut Wisdom

Days at Stillmeadow now have the quality of lyric poetry. They sing with color. The whole valley is a garden, for the meadows are starred with daisies, day lilies bloom along winding roads, and roses cascade over fences.

When we came to Stillmeadow, the yard was a hayfield; the garden, a tangle of weeds and briars. But in June, day lilies began to bloom all over, lifting tawny cornucopias in great profusion. They seemed like a message of hope for us. When Jill, my housemate, tried to separate them, she had so many that she threw some clumps in the swamp and some on her compost heap. They all bloomed riotously the next June. Their vigor is incredible. They even grew under the giant sugar maples, and still do, all these years later. They are lovely in the house, but each bloom lasts just a day, so bouquets of them are not a lazy woman's job. But in a copper jug on an old trestle table they are very special.

Now picnic time begins, and this is picnic country. The state has many roadside picnic spots with tables and benches and stone fireplaces, called romantically Maple Rest or Frog Rock or White Oak. But all you need to do is to drive down any country road and stop by a nameless bubbling brook and unpack the basket. There are woodsy places and countless lakes and ponds and hilltops with rolling countryside spread below. There are deserted pastures with rock ledges outcropping.

At the market, buns and rolls and frankfurters and hamburgers are bought endlessly. They are basic for Americans in summer. I note that when I ask the grandchildren what they want, they alternate hamburgers and frankfurters. I tell myself that both foods are protein and nourishing. And they are certainly easier than fried chicken!

The cockers and the Irish setter like June best of all, I think. Days are not hot and twilights are pleasant. The lawn is just right for digging, and the air is full of birds to bark at. Moonlight nights are full of wonderful scents and mysterious sounds. Also I stay outdoors more, and the boy comes to mow the lawn and toss things for the dogs, and weekends the children play games with them. Life is just one long social occasion. Holly's favorite job is helping hang out the laundry. There's always a sock that gets dropped, and she pounces and carries it off and tosses it in the air. This is one reason there are

so many unmatched socks at Stillmeadow. Odd ones turn up under the mock-orange bush or tucked in the stone wall or in the wisteria. Holly has not lost them; she has put them away.

Holly has one habit none of the others has. If she wants to go out, she asks politely first. If I say, "Just let me finish this sentence," she eyes me briefly, then utters a firm bark. It is a special bark, reasonable and muted. Then she brings me a slipper and whacks it against my knee. Then she gets let out. If she decides to go out in the night (full moon), she nuzzles me while thumping her tail against the bed. Next she puts both forepaws on my arm, pressing firmly. Finally she picks up my slipper and taps it against me slowly, then faster and faster. Then she precedes me to the door, presenting me with my slipper at the threshold. I stand at the door and watch her pause by the well house, turning her head as she air-scents. Then she is off, for 20 minutes or so, in the white light of the moon, her tail a banner behind her. Returning, she barks at the door and dashes in—and in five minutes is fast asleep.

Gladys Taber

Hometown ISSUE ideals

Ideals' Pages from the Past

On the following six pages we are presenting a selection from Hometown Ideals 1952.

Home Town . . .

Lynda Schlomann

Where people meet with outstretched hands,
   And grins upon their faces;
Where songs and laughter seem to blend
   More than at other places.

Where footsteps seem a little lighter
   As they fall upon the street,
And eyes shine a little brighter
   When they chance to meet.

Where the sun shines a little more,
   And the grass seems always green;
Where the bird's song is always sweeter
   Than anywhere I've been.

Where the rain feels a bit more gentle
   As it comes falling down,
Upon the roofs and sidewalks —
   Of my home town.

Sunset Fairy

Richie T. Weikel

Have I ever told the story
Of the Sunset Fairy bright,
Whom I found beside my lily pool
In a most distressing plight?

She had dropped her pot of colors
Used to paint the sunset sky,
Into my spacious garden
From a cloud as she passed by.

She cried, "The pot rolled from the cloud
And fell into your bed of flowers,
And now, instead of sunshine,
We will have gray skies and showers!"

I said, "Don't worry, fairy, dear,
I'll help you find that pot you bet,
So you can hurry on your way
And per schedule we'll have sunset!"

She looked among the daisies,
While I searched the bed of phlox.
Alas, we found the pot quite empty,
Splashed o'er our stately hollyhocks.

That is why they are variegated,
White, yellow, red and pink;
And from my bedroom window,
Look lovely, don't you think?

The Fairies' Party

L. O. Vermillion

Yes, the fairies held a party
In my garden one balmy night,
Placed their jackets in the tulips,
While they danced in bright moon light;

The gentle breezes rocked them,
While I watched them, all unseen,
As they danced among the flowers,
And on the velvet lawn so green.

There they played with lights and shadows
Until the early break of day,
Then they gathered up their babies
And they quietly stole away.

Then came bees and butterflies
And a bright green humming bird,
I know not how they knew it,
Or who had spread the word

Of the beauty left on petals
And perfume that filled the air,
Or the nectar left in blossoms
Just for them and me to share.

Mother Love

Henry B. Knox

There's only one in all the world
Whose "Mother-love" we claim,
And though we've often grieved her heart
That love remains the same.

A mother's love — oh, who would dare
To measure what 'tis worth
To each of us to know the love
Of her who gave us birth.

A love which follows all the way
Our footsteps here or yon;
A love, although rebuffed sometimes,
Persists in loving on.

A sacrificial love which bears
The heartaches and the pain,
Depriving self for those it loves,
Yet never doth complain.

How oft we fail to comprehend
Our mother's love until
That place is vacant here below
Which no one else can fill.

For God hath placed in Mother's heart
A jewel from above
For which there is no substitute,
And called it "MOTHER-LOVE".

Midsummer Pause

There is a moment in midsummer when the earth
pauses between flower and fruit; the hay is cut,
the oats ripen, on pasture knolls pearly everlasting
lifts its small fountains of silver and gold.

The skies are blue, the hills rest all day
like men at noon under a shady tree.
The leaves have turned dark green, they hoard
their strength, no strong wind harms them.

Boys swim under the big elm by the crick.
Locusts drone in the trees; the swallows
gather on wires, and starlings in flocks
wheel over the meadows like curving hands.

Fred Lape

MIDSUMMER PAUSE from BARNYARD YEAR by Fred Lape.
Copyright 1950 by Fred Lape. Reprinted by permission of
Harper & Row, Publishers, Inc.

Coming in Homespun Ideals

A tribute to John Wayne, an American hero . . .
a special feature on the Isle of Man Millennium
Year 1979 . . . a look at the Edison phonograph
. . . an excerpt from "The Great Stone Face" by
Nathaniel Hawthorne . . . Ideals Best-Loved
Poet, Alice Leedy Mason . . . Pages from the
Past, School Ideals, 1949 . . . plus poetry and
prose illustrating the beauty of summer.

ACKNOWLEDGMENTS

THIS BEING THE MIDDLE OF JUNE . . . by May Allread Baker. From THE GIFT OF
THE YEAR by May Allread Baker. Copyright © 1964 by The Brethren Press, Elgin,
Illinois. Used by permission. THE QUIET GRANDEUR OF THE PETRIFIED FOREST.
Excerpted from PETRIFIED FOREST, THE STORY BEHIND THE SCENERY. Re-
printed through courtesy of Petrified Forest Museum Association, Arizona. THE
CLOVER; THE DAYS GONE BY; MORNING; THE OLD SWIMMIN' HOLE by James
Whitcomb Riley. From THE BEST LOVED POEMS AND BALLADS OF JAMES
WHITCOMB RILEY published by The Bobbs-Merrill Company. A SUMMER DAY by
Garnett Ann Schultz. From SOMETHING BEAUTIFUL by Garnett Ann Schultz.
Copyright © 1966 by Garnett Ann Schultz. Published by Dorrance & Company. THE
SWING; WHERE GO THE BOATS?; THE WIND by Robert Louis Stevenson. From A
CHILD'S GARDEN OF VERSES by Robert Louis Stevenson (Charles Scribner's Sons,
1917). Our sincere thanks to the following authors whose addresses we were unable to
locate: Gwen Castle for O PERFECT DAY; Harry Kemp for TELL ALL THE WORLD;
Elsie K. Pierce for CAREFREE WAY.

Additional Photo Credits: Front cover, Four by Five. Inside front cover, Freelance
Photographers Guild. Inside back cover, Corinth Center, Vermont, Alpha Photo
Associates. Back cover, Bruce Coleman.

SUBSCRIBE TO IDEALS TODAY!

SAVE 33% OFF the single issue cost of the inspiring magazine that celebrates traditional American family values!

Featuring •
full color photography and illustrations • poetry and prose by our nation's finest writers • homespun verse by our own readers • fascinating articles on cooking, crafts, collectibles and travel • lively profiles of famous Americans • fireside wisdom to lift the spirit and touch the heart

All without any advertising!

So don't delay! Mail the postage-paid coupon below today!

☐ Please enter my 1-year subscription (8 issues) for only $15.95—a savings of $7.65 off the single issue price.

☐ Please enter my 2-year subscription (16 issues) for only $27.95—a saving of $11.45 off the single issue price.

Outside Continental U.S. - Add $2.00 Per Subscription Year For Postage & Handling

( ) Bill me. ( ) I enclose check/money order in separate envelope.

Please charge: ( ) Master Charge ( ) BA/Visa

Exp. Date _____ Bank _____

Card # _____

Signature _____

NAME _____

ADDRESS _____

CITY _____ STATE_____ ZIP _____
CO96

SUBSCRIBE TO IDEALS TODAY!

SAVE 33% OFF the single issue cost of the inspiring magazine that celebrates traditional American family values!

Featuring •
full color photography and illustrations • poetry and prose by our nation's finest writers • homespun verse by our own readers • fascinating articles on cooking, crafts, collectibles and travel • lively profiles of famous Americans • fireside wisdom to lift the spirit and touch the heart

All without any advertising!

So don't delay! Mail the postage-paid coupon below today!

☐ Please enter my 1-year subscription (8 issues) for only $15.95—a savings of $7.65 off the single issue price.

☐ Please enter my 2-year subscription (16 issues) for only $27.95—a saving of $11.45 off the single issue price.

Outside Continental U.S. - Add $2.00 Per Subscription Year For Postage & Handling

( ) Bill me. ( ) I enclose check/money order in separate envelope.

Please charge: ( ) Master Charge ( ) BA/Visa

Exp. Date _____ Bank _____

Card # _____

Signature _____

NAME _____

ADDRESS _____

CITY _____ STATE_____ ZIP _____
CO96

 # AN IDEAL GIFT

for all seasons . . . and loved ones of all ages!

SAVE 33% OFF THE SINGLE ISSUE PRICE

So don't delay! Mail the postage-paid coupon below today!

( ) Please send a 1 year subscription to IDEALS (8 issues for $15.95) a savings of $7.65 off the single issue price—to my special friend or relative listed below.

( ) Please send a 2 year subscription to IDEALS (16 issues for $27.95) a savings of $11.45 off the single issue price—to my special friend or relative listed below.

Outside Continental U.S. - Add $2.00 Per Subscription Year For Postage & Handling

Gift Name _____

Address _____

City _____ State_____ Zip _____

Sign gift card from: _____

Address _____

City _____ State_____ Zip _____

( ) Bill me. ( ) I enclose check/money order in separate envelope.

Please charge: ( ) Master Charge ( ) BA/Visa

Exp. Date _____ Bank _____

Card # _____

Signature _____
CO96

 # AN IDEAL GIFT

for all seasons . . . and loved ones of all ages!

SAVE 33% OFF THE SINGLE ISSUE PRICE

So don't delay! Mail the postage-paid coupon below today!

( ) Please send a 1 year subscription to IDEALS (8 issues for $15.95) a savings of $7.65 off the single issue price—to my special friend or relative listed below.

( ) Please send a 2 year subscription to IDEALS (16 issues for $27.95) a savings of $11.45 off the single issue price—to my special friend or relative listed below.

Outside Continental U.S. - Add $2.00 Per Subscription Year For Postage & Handling

Gift Name _____

Address _____

City _____ State_____ Zip _____

Sign gift card from: _____

Address _____

City _____ State_____ Zip _____

( ) Bill me. ( ) I enclose check/money order in separate envelope.

Please charge: ( ) Master Charge ( ) BA/Visa

Exp. Date _____ Bank _____

Card # _____

Signature _____
CO96

FIRST CLASS
PERMIT NO. 5761
MILWAUKEE,
WISCONSIN

BUSINESS REPLY MAIL
No postage stamp necessary if mailed in the United States

POSTAGE WILL BE PAID BY

ideals
PUBLISHING CORPORATION
11315 WATERTOWN PLANK RD.
MILWAUKEE, WISCONSIN 53226

FIRST CLASS
PERMIT NO. 5761
MILWAUKEE,
WISCONSIN

BUSINESS REPLY MAIL
No postage stamp necessary if mailed in the United States

POSTAGE WILL BE PAID BY

ideals
PUBLISHING CORPORATION
11315 WATERTOWN PLANK RD.
MILWAUKEE, WISCONSIN 53226

FIRST CLASS
PERMIT NO. 5761
MILWAUKEE,
WISCONSIN

BUSINESS REPLY MAIL
No postage stamp necessary if mailed in the United States

POSTAGE WILL BE PAID BY

ideals
PUBLISHING CORPORATION
11315 WATERTOWN PLANK RD.
MILWAUKEE, WISCONSIN 53226

FIRST CLASS
PERMIT NO. 5761
MILWAUKEE,
WISCONSIN

BUSINESS REPLY MAIL
No postage stamp necessary if mailed in the United States

POSTAGE WILL BE PAID BY

ideals
PUBLISHING CORPORATION
11315 WATERTOWN PLANK RD.
MILWAUKEE, WISCONSIN 53226